Pets at the Vet

Elaine McKinnon

illustrated by
Anita Morra

PowerKiDS press

New York

Published in 2017 by The Rosen Publishing Group, Inc.
29 East 21st Street, New York, NY 10010

First Edition

Managing Editor: Nathalie Beullens-Maoui
Editor: Caitie McAneney
Book Design: Michael Flynn
Illustrator: Anita Morra

Library of Congress Cataloging-in-Publication Data

Names: McKinnon, Elaine, author.
Title: Pets at the vet / Elaine McKinnon.
Description: New York : PowerKids Press, [2017] | Series: Community helpers |
  Includes index.
Identifiers: LCCN 2016027639| ISBN 9781499427066 (pbk. book) | ISBN
  9781499427073 (6 pack) | ISBN 9781499430325 (library bound book)
Subjects: LCSH: Veterinarians–Juvenile literature. | Veterinary
  medicine–Juvenile literature. | Dogs–Health–Juvenile literature.
Classification: LCC SF756 .M296 2017 | DDC 636.089–dc23
LC record available at https://lccn.loc.gov/2016027639

Manufactured in the United States of America

CPSIA Compliance Information: Batch #BW17PK: For Further Information contact Rosen Publishing, New York, New York at 1-800-237-9932

Contents

My dog's name is Copper.

It's time for his checkup.
We go to the vet!

Time to go!

6

Copper loves car rides.

There are many dogs in
the waiting room.

There are cats, too.
Copper makes new friends.

The vet calls our name.

It's Copper's turn.

The vet puts Copper on a scale.

That tells how much he weighs.

The vet puts Copper on a table.
She looks at his ears and mouth.

Copper licks her face!

The vet looks at Copper's fur and skin.

She listens to his hea

The vet clips Copper's nails.

They were getting long!

The vet says Copper is healthy!

She gives him healthy treats.

The vet helps
animals every day.

I want to be a vet someday!

Words to Know

dog

scale

treat

Index